MELANIE MOSHER

Fire Pie Trout

Illustrated by RENNÉ BENOIT

FIFTH
HOUSE

Published in Canada by Fifth House Publishers, 195 Allstate Parkway, Markham, ON, L3R 4T8 www.fitzhenry.ca

Published in the U.S. by Fifth House Publishers, 311 Washington Street, Brighton, Massachusetts 02135

We acknowledge with thanks the Canada Council for the Arts, and the Ontario Arts Council for their support of our publishing program. We acknowledge the financial support of the Government of Canada through the Canada Book Fund (CBF) for our publishing activities.

Library and Archives Canada Cataloguing in Publication
Mosher, Melanie, author
        Fire pie trout / Melanie Mosher ; illustrations by Renné Benoit.
ISBN 978-1-927083-18-5 (bound)
        I. Benoit, Renné, illustrator II. Title.
PS8626.O84265F67 2014   jC813'.6   C2014-901309-4

Publisher Cataloging-in-Publication Data (U.S.)
Mosher, Melanie.
    Fire pie trout / Melanie Mosher ; illustrated by Renné Benoit.
[24] pages : col. ill. ; cm.
Summary: Through a fishing trip with her grandfather, a young girl discovers that she can conquer her deepest fears: of the dark, of scary movies, and of trying new things she has never tried before.
ISBN-13: 978-1-92708-318-5
1. Families – Juvenile fiction. 2. Grandfathers – Juvenile fiction.
3. Fear in children – Juvenile fiction. I. Benoit, Renné. II. Title.
[E] de23 PZ7.M684fi 2014

Text and cover design by Kong Njo
Cover illustration by Renné Benoit

Printed and bound in China by Sheck Wah Tong Printing Press Ltd.

"Grampie?" asked Grace.

"Yes, Gracie," answered Gramps.

"Guess what! I packed our favourite lunch."

"FIRE PIE!"

"Right! PIZZA," said Grace.